BY DENNIS HASELEY

Dr. Gravity

Shadows

Ghost Catcher

The Thieves' Market

My Father Doesn't Know
About the Woods and Me

The Counterfeiter

The Cave of Snores

Kite Flier

The Soap Bandit

The Scared One

The Pirate Who Tried
to Capture the Moon

The Old Banjo

SHADOWS

Dennis Haseley

SHADOWS

Pictures by Leslie Bowman

A Sunburst Book
Farrar Straus Giroux

For Claudia

D . H .

For my friend Janice

L . B .

Text copyright © 1991 by Dennis Haseley
Pictures copyright © 1991 by Leslie Bowman
All rights reserved
Library of Congress catalog card number: 90-56149
Published in Canada by HarperCollins*CanadaLtd*
Printed in the United States of America
First edition, 1991
Sunburst edition, 1993

SHADOWS

I DON'T KNOW how, but this is what happened, so I'll tell it. But first, I'll turn off the lights, so there's just this small one lit.

Now, watch my hands. Behind them, see that shadow on the wall. That's Tobias, the dog. And see, when I make a space between my thumb and forefinger, it's like his mouth is opening. And closing. And opening. And see, when I put my hands down, dog Tobias is gone.

Although I'm not so sure. I'm not so sure he doesn't have a mind of his own and he isn't hiding somewhere, or off running through the night the way he did once before.

I'll keep just the small light on while I tell it.

3

1

IT USED TO BE, I could never make my hands work right. Not for most of that summer when I lived with my aunt and uncle. But Grandpa could.

My aunt and uncle didn't have children of their own, but they had tried to fix up the room where I was staying so a kid would like it. Uncle Edward had put up a picture with some hunters in it, pointing their guns in the air. Way off in the distance there were some geese, in the shape of a V. Aunt Elena had put a stuffed clown on the dresser, but I'd noticed in the week I'd been there he'd never sit up right; his head would always roll forward like he was falling asleep.

I was staring through the window, watching the meadow beyond the fence that Uncle Edward

5

had built. He said sometimes you could see a deer there. I was watching it grow darker, thinking how it seemed a little darker in my room than in the sky and the meadow. And I was wondering about my mother. Wondering what she was doing right now. Maybe eating food in one of those diners, that's what she'd called them in the letter she'd written me. I was wishing I was with her and she could give me her roll, like she always did when we were out.

Then I heard a board creak in the floor behind me. I turned quickly and saw a man there and called out.

"What are you scared of, boy?" he said.

"You," I said. He was standing in the half-light, and he had a big mustache coming down around his mouth. It was hard to make all of him out in the darkness, but he seemed pretty big. A lot bigger than me.

"You shouldn't be scared of me. I'm your grandpa."

"You look like a pirate to me."

He liked that. He put his head back and started laughing, even though I hadn't meant it to be funny.

"That's a good one," he said. "A pirate. A pirate in West Virginia." He laughed some more, and then he walked over to me. "They said you'd be asleep, but I wanted to get a look at ya."

He took a match case out of his pocket, and drew a match across the iron frame of the bed where I was sitting. He held it up to me and stared at me for a moment. He seemed to see something that he liked, because he smiled. Then he took a candle down from a shelf and put it on the table next to my bed.

I took a look at him, too, while he lit the candle. His face had lots of lines in it, like a map that's been folded again and again.

He sat on the bed next to me. "Whatcha doin' up so late?" he asked.

"Just lookin' around."

"See much?"

"Nope," I said.

He thought about that for a second. Then he said, "Seen that shadow behind you on the wall?"

I turned around quickly. A large dark shadow of me, sent by the candlelight, was on the wall behind my head.

"You've got one, too," I said. I pointed.

He turned. "Well, that does look like a pirate's head, don't it?" he said, and smiled. "Now just keep lookin' at the wall."

I looked behind me again. Suddenly I saw the shadow of a hawk!

I glanced back at him. His hands—tough old hands like tree stumps—were twisted together.

"Now don't be lookin' here," he said. "Look at the wall."

So I turned toward the wall again. The hawk started to move its wings—gently, the way a hawk does—and it was soaring on my wall as if it were soaring through a patch of sky.

Then the hawk disappeared. I looked back at him, and his hands were in his lap. He was looking at me.

"I'm keeping you up too late," he said. "You probably got enough to get used to."

"I guess so," I said. He started to get up. "But I am wondering about something," I said.

"What's that?" He was looking at me.

"Does he have a name?"

Now he smiled. "Well, sure," he said. I looked back at the wall, and the hawk was there again. "This here hawk is named Derek," Grandpa said. "And Derek can soar so high he can leave the earth far behind. Till there's just blue sky and clouds, above him and below him."

I saw the shadow of the head of the hawk move a little and look down. This way, and that.

"And his eyes are so sharp he can see everything. So when he gets hungry, he can spot a fish—way below—and dive into a stream for it."

Now, on the wall, the shadow's head moved, and the hawk streaked downward. As it neared the bottom of the wall, its tail went down and

its legs came out with sharp claws. Then I couldn't see it anymore.

"Where'd he go?"

"You can't see him now, he's in the stream," Grandpa said.

"Did he catch the fish?"

"I don't know yet."

After a while, Derek flew back up, shaking his head and his wings. His talons were empty.

"He didn't catch it?" I asked.

"It was just a small one," said Grandpa. "He let it get away."

Derek was up in the sky again, floating. Looking.

I turned and snuck a glance at Grandpa. He wasn't looking at Derek now. He was looking at me again. At me and the shadow on the wall behind me.

"Grandpa," I said.

"That's right," he said. "You know, you look like another little boy I knew once."

"Who was that?"

"I'll tell you sometime," he said.

I looked back at the wall. At the hawk's shadow, and my shadow.

Then Derek disappeared. Grandpa said even hawks had to sleep. He said he'd see me again, soon enough. Then he blew out the candle and he left. The room smelled like him, a sweet smell of old wood, for a while after he'd gone.

I lay in my bed and looked at my blank wall. There was still some light coming in from the outside. And for a second, I could see like Derek. From way up high, with my stomach dropping out, I could see this little room I was in, in this house in West Virginia where I'd never been before. I could see my grandfather moving along a dark road, through the June night. And way up North and East, I could make out a big town, with brightly lit lights in all the windows, and signs, and diners filled with people. And I could see my mother finishing her meal.

She had put her roll aside.

2

SINCE I WAS staying with them, I was helping out Aunt Elena and Uncle Edward in the secondhand furniture and odds-and-ends store they ran. My first week there they'd shown me what they wanted me to do: polish up the old dressers and bookcases they kept on the second floor with something that seemed to be a combination of paint and shiner; fetch things for Aunt Elena when she was showing something to someone; count up stuff like pot holders and pieces of silverware to let her know how many she had.

But in the days after I met Grandpa, I wasn't thinking too much about my chores, even though they were giving me spending money for doing them. I was twisting my hands together, trying to make them into the shape of a bird. I was looking in the corners and by the edges of the windows upstairs, looking for a place where I could make a shadow, even in the middle of the day.

I heard the tinkle of the bell on the door from downstairs. If it was the postman, he might have one of my mother's letters. But it was only two o'clock; he never usually came till four.

I peeked down the steps. If I looked right along the railing, I could spy whoever had come into the shop. This was a tall lady I hadn't seen before. But Aunt Elena sure seemed happy to see her. Her face broke into a smile, and then she turned and called up the stairs.

"Jamie. Jamie honey."

I wanted to tell her that I had never in my life been called Jamie honey.

I waited a couple of seconds, so she wouldn't know I was spying, and then I came down the stairs.

"Why, he's a big boy," the tall woman said.

"He's a big help around here," said Aunt Elena, smiling at me.

"Well, how do you do," said the tall woman. "My name is Mrs. Bishop. And you sure are a big boy."

"How do you do, ma'am," I said.

"Mrs. Bishop is one of my oldest friends," said Aunt Elena. "Although it seems I never see enough of you."

"Yes, it does," said Mrs. Bishop. "And how long is he here for?" she asked my aunt.

"Oh, just for the summer," said Aunt Elena. "I must have told you, he and his mother are moving out from where they've lived in Illinois. She's looking for a job, up East, in Connecticut."

"All on her own?" said Mrs. Bishop. I didn't know why she sounded that way all of a sudden.

"Well, she has someone there, an aunt, I believe, who's quite advanced in years. But no one who can really keep a close eye on a boy." She opened her eyes a little wider when she said that, like there was a lot more in what she was saying. "We're just glad she came to that herself."

"I should think so."

"So, until she's settled in, he's staying with us."

Mrs. Bishop nodded. Then she turned to me. "Well, I bet you like it around here, don't you, Jamie?"

"Oh, I do," I said. "I truly do."

"And you'll mind your aunt and uncle?"

"I will," I said.

She nodded like she was satisfied with me.

"You go finish up your chores now," said my aunt.

"Yes, ma'am."

"He is the image of his father," Mrs. Bishop said as I was walking away.

"Oh, I don't know," said my aunt.

I stayed for a minute again, back at the top of the stairs, listening.

"Such a shame that was," said Mrs. Bishop.

"Yes, such a shame," said my aunt. "The boy's mother can hardly talk about it to this day."

"He does seem a quiet one, though," said Mrs. Bishop.

"Yes, we must be grateful for that," said my aunt. She looked around the store without saying anything for a while. Then she started talking about all the rain they'd been having, and how it looked so bad for the crops.

I moved away, and I found what I was looking for. The sun struck a mirror on the top of a big pine dresser, and the sunlight reflected back against the wall in the shape of a window. When I put up my hand, it cast a shadow.

I tried to remember again how Grandpa's hands had looked. I twisted mine together, the way I thought he'd done. But the shadow came out like some forsaken creature, with one wing coming out of its back.

I'd have to see Grandpa soon. I'd have to get him to show me how he'd made that hawk soaring on my wall.

3

LATER THAT AFTERNOON, after the postman dropped off some circulars, I started the long walk to where my aunt and uncle lived. From the store it was about three miles by the road. The road ran along a river until it reached a bridge; then the road went over and back along the water, back along the way it had already come, but on the other side of the river. My uncle said if he could ever learn to jump the thirty feet over that water he could save a lot of time. It was funny, though; the only time he seemed to jump was when Aunt Elena called him.

When I was about a half mile from the bridge, I saw some kids down off the side of the road, on the bank. There were two boys and a girl. One of the boys looked a couple years older than the other two kids. They were staring at the river, at a big tree that had fallen across it from the other side. The log made a kind of a bridge. The water lapped up against its side, and sometimes ran over it.

The kids looked at me, and then they looked back at the log, except the older boy. He kept staring at me. I kept walking until I was on the road right by where they were standing, a little below me.

"Who are you?" said the older boy. The other boy and girl looked up at me.

"My name's Jamie," I said.

"Never seen you before."

"That's 'cause I'm new here," I said.

"Where you livin'?" he asked.

"With my aunt and uncle."

"Where's your mama?"

"Up North, looking for work," I said.

The little girl picked up a stone and threw it into the river. Then the younger boy threw in a stick.

"Where's your dad?"

"He died," I said.

The girl looked up and stared at me. The boy did, too.

"How'd it happen?" asked the older boy.

"In a fire," I said. "At the plant."

"At the *plant*," the boy said, and grinned. One

of his top teeth was crooked. "You mean like a tomato *plant*?"

"Factory," I said. "Wasn't his fault. He almost saved a bunch of people." I started to walk along the road. "It was a long time ago." My face felt hot.

The older boy seemed to be thinking about what I'd told him.

"Hey," he said. "Wait."

I stopped and looked down at him. They were all looking up at me again.

"You going to the bridge?" he asked.

"Of course I am," I said.

"Why don't you take the bridge here?" he said.

I looked to where he was pointing. It was the big log fallen across the river. I looked back at them. They were all staring at me, waiting to see what I'd do.

"It ain't *deep*," said the other boy.

I walked back, and then down the bank toward the log. I skidded on a couple of stones on the slope, but I pretended not to notice. The three of them moved away as I approached the log.

When I put my foot on it, it seemed to move, but I couldn't be sure. There were flashes in the middle of the river, where it flowed over rocks. I thought about what my mother would say if she could see me now: how I should never be careless, that was the worst thing. I lifted my other foot and put it on the log. And if I ever were, I must be sure to tell her, or somebody, because that was the next worst thing, not telling what was true. My heart was pounding.

I was sure now, the log had moved.

I jumped back onto the shore.

The older boy grinned. The other two just watched me.

"I don't like this old bridge," I said. Then I

turned and walked back up onto the road. I
didn't look back. I didn't look back until I had
walked awhile, and then I heard the older boy
call me.

"Hey, Jamie," he said.

I stopped and turned around. The three of
them were walking, way out on the log, with
their arms out. Walking carefully, but walking,
barefoot, over the middle of the river.

I could tell the older boy was grinning.

4

GRANDPA DIDN'T come that day. He didn't come the following day, or the next, or the next after that. I asked Aunt Elena about it one morning at breakfast. She said he lived about four miles beyond the store. And he didn't have a car, just a horse and wagon.

"And besides," she said, "he's old."

"He's not," I said.

In the meantime, another Sunday came. Uncle Edward called me into his and Aunt Elena's room and held up a large black suit. You could pretend it was the shadow of a man.

"Do you know what this is for?" he asked.

"For going to church again?" I said.

"Yes, but more than that. This Sunday it's my

turn to be a deacon. A deacon is somebody who helps out the minister. There's lots of fellows who want to do that, so we take turns. Now what do you think of that?"

"That's real good," I said. I tried to sound like I meant it. And then I reached up and touched the cloth of the suit.

Their church was pretty much the same as the church back home, except the people talked back a little more when the minister spoke. During the service, Uncle Edward stuck a basket on a long pole down the aisles, for people to drop their money in.

Afterward, the minister called him up to stand with him at the door and shake people's hands as they left.

When Aunt Elena and I reached him, he introduced me to the minister.

"This is Jamie," said Uncle Edward. He was smiling real wide, and his face was all red, up to the top of his head, where he was bald.

"Well, how do you do," said the minister, and he leaned over and shook my hand.

"This is old Darcy's grandson," said Uncle Edward. "William's son."

"You don't say," said the minister.

"You probably never thought there'd be a day when his boy would be sitting in your pew," said Uncle Edward. "I recall the only time you'd see him in church was if you looked out the window and seen him on that mare of his."

"He had a mare?" I said.

"Now, Edward," said Aunt Elena. Nobody said anything for a second.

"We do expect he'll be a teacher when he grows up," said Aunt Elena. "Same as his mama."

It was the first I'd heard of it.

"Where is the boy's mother?" asked the minister.

Now Aunt Elena was blushing. "She's— why—she's up looking for work. She just has to. And she specially asked us to take care of him."

"Well, that's fine, then," said the minister.

The next day I got two letters from my mother. The postmarks said different dates, and Aunt Elena explained that sometimes that happens with the mail. My mother said she knew I was minding Aunt Elena and not doing anything she wouldn't want me to do. She said there were a couple of jobs teaching school that looked good— she used the word "promising," like when you promise someone something—and she said they weren't like the job she'd had in Illinois, where the money had run out and all the kids had to transfer to the school in the next town. She said there were more cars than you could imagine on the streets, and that nearly everyone had electric lights.

In my letter, I told her everything was fine.

The next night, Grandpa came again.

I always tried to stay awake, to listen for his horse and wagon. Even though I'd never seen it, I thought I'd know what it would sound like. That night, I didn't hear a horse, just the rumble of an automobile. But the next minute, Grandpa was standing in my doorway.

"Where's your horse?" I asked him.

"I gave him the night off," said Grandpa, coming toward where I was sitting on my bed. "I got a ride up with Mr. McCall."

"I guess you'll have to stay awhile," I said.

He looked at me. "I will," he said. "Your Aunt Elena and Uncle Ed have a cot for me in their sitting room. But I'll be going back in the morning."

"I guess you've got lots to do," I said.

"Oh, yessiree." He laughed. "Especially now."

"What's now?" I asked.

"Now that you're here. I've got lots of practicing to do."

"With the shadows?"

"With the shadows," he said.

He took down the candle and lit it. I looked

over at the wall, at our two shadows, the big one and the small one.

"Can you walk on a tree trunk?" I asked.

"Not if it's standing up straight," he said, and smiled.

"I mean if it's over."

"Sure," he said. But he looked at me like he didn't understand.

"I can't," I said. And then I told him about what had happened with the kids.

He listened, and he didn't say anything for a while. Then he said, "Same thing happened to that other little boy I knew."

"It did?"

"Couldn't walk a log. Afraid of climbing trees, even. Afraid of stepping stones over a brook. That's because he'd never met Robert."

"Who's Robert?" I asked.

"You'll meet him soon enough," he said. "But after he met Robert, he could *dance* on a log if he wanted. Why . . . he even became a log roller . . . rolled logs down the big rivers. He could climb a tree with one hand, he could—"

"—he could balance on a mare," I said.

"That's right," he said. After a second, he looked at the wall as if he saw something. I turned and looked, and I saw the shadow of a big cat on the wall.

"Who's that?" I asked. I didn't turn around and look at his hands this time.

"That's Robert, the bobcat," said Grandpa. "How are you, Robert?" he said to the shadow.

The shadow flicked its ears. Then it slowly turned its head and looked at him. Then at me.

Then, faster than I could follow, it sprang onto the corner of the wall.

"How'd you make him do that?" I asked.

"I don't always make him," said Grandpa. "Sometimes he's got a mind of his own."

The shadow jumped back into the middle of the wall.

"Robert's on a real narrow branch right now," said Grandpa in a quiet voice.

I watched the shadow move one paw slowly in front of the next.

"He's got the best balance of all," said Grandpa. "And he's smart, too." The shadow put his paw out and felt in the air like he was feeling a bending twig. Then he drew back and tried another way. "He knows where it's dangerous and where it's not."

"He wouldn't have any problems on a log," I said.

"That's right," said Grandpa.

Robert finished his walk on the branch. Then he sat down and licked his paws and ran them over his face and ears.

"That's what a house cat does," I said.

"Yes, it is," said Grandpa. "But it's what a bobcat does, too. Make no mistake about it, Robert's a wild one."

Suddenly the cat sprang away and was gone.

"He just saw the shadow of a chipmunk," said Grandpa, and laughed.

I turned around. His hands were lying in his lap.

"Will you show me?" I asked.

"Sure," he said. "But remember, they're tricky to figure out at first."

He took my hands in his and arranged my

fingers this way and that. Then he held them up to the light. On the wall, the shadow of the bobcat sprang into place.

"There he is," said Grandpa.

"Robert," I said. He hadn't been there, and now he looked so right all of a sudden, it seemed like the real shadow of a cat. I glanced behind me, at the candle, like I expected to see one there. Then back at the wall.

"Where'd you learn them?" I asked. My voice was low.

"I can't rightly say." He was holding my hands, and we were both staring at that shadow now. We were holding still, like when you see a deer walk by. Then he let my hands go. The shadow changed, and looked less like an animal.

I stared at it, waiting for it to come back. "Doesn't look like Robert now," I said.

"Oh, it's Robert, all right," said Grandpa. "It's just that, at first, they aren't clear. It's like you're seeing them from some distance. Same thing happened to me."

"When will they get clearer?"

"When they get closer," he said. Now he was smiling. "It won't be long."

"And then I'll get it?" I said.

"And then you'll get it," he said.

5

ALL MORNING, I'd been sitting on the floor, upstairs at the store, where the sun reflected off a mirror. I'd been trying to make Robert. I'd been trying to make Derek's wings. But my hands had gotten all twisted up.

There was a long, narrow bookcase next to a table. I climbed from a chair to the tabletop, and was able to get up to it without too much trouble. It wasn't really so narrow, but I was pretending it was, as thin as a branch where I had to put one foot slowly before the other. I had my arms straight out. I didn't hear Aunt Elena until she'd walked up close. Then I saw her and quickly got down the way I'd come up.

She was shaking her head, as if she couldn't believe what she'd seen.

28

"You know," she said, and then stopped and took a breath. "You know you could fall, and God knows what, doing things like that up here."

"Yes, ma'am." I wanted to tell her it wasn't so narrow as all that, but I didn't say anything.

"You know, Jamie," she said. "Jamie honey. When people are reckless, well, or high-spirited, they can get away with it for a while. Especially if—" She stopped for a second; she seemed upset. "Especially if they get encouraged, do you get what I mean?"

"If people tell them it's good," I said.

"That's right," she said. "Or admire them for it. But you can't get away with it forever," she said. "It always catches up, in the end." She was looking at me funny, as if she was seeing someone else there for a minute, someone else she was trying to talk to.

"I was just walking on the bookshelf," I said.

She took a moment. "I know," she said. "I know." She looked like she was ready to walk away and then thought better of it. "But what got into you to try that?"

"It was nothing," I said. "Just Grandpa and me were talking."

"I guess I might have known." She looked over at where I was supposed to be working. It was a whole area of furniture, pushed close to-gether, so it looked like one big tabletop. Only a little part of it was shiny.

"You best be getting back to work," she said.

The next time Grandpa came, I told him I was having trouble making the shadows. He and I walked out to the front porch. By the light of a lantern, I showed him what I could do.

Then I put my hands down. "It's not any good," I said.

"It's always like that at first," he said. "They're still far away."

"Fifty miles," I said.

He lit his pipe. We looked out at the small front yard, at the wheelbarrow with its handles in the air.

"Maybe you should meet Tobias," he said.

"Tobias?"

He nodded toward the front wall of the house, where the lantern light shone on the wood. I saw the head and front legs of a large dog appear.

"Part wolf was Tobias," said Grandpa. "But mostly dog."

The shadow head cocked to the side and whimpered a little.

"Yes, Tobias, I'll tell young Jamie here all about you."

The head lifted, the mouth opened and closed quickly, as if he was barking.

"He likes to have his story told," said Grandpa.

"What's his story?" I asked.

"Tobias was the mascot of a whole regiment of soldiers. He drilled with them. He stayed up on guard duty, to keep the night sentinel company, while the other soldiers slept."

I saw the dog shadow cock his head and look at Grandpa.

"He wants me to get to the good part," said Grandpa.

"One night, the soldiers walked into an enemy ambush. Even Tobias hadn't smelled the enemy, who had covered themselves with mud, so they couldn't be seen."

The dog shadow hung his head for a moment.

"Maybe you could pet him," said Grandpa.

I put my hand out, until the shadow of it was just above the shadow dog. He lifted his nose up, like he was a real dog, nuzzling my hand.

"For three days and nights, they were pinned down by enemy fire. They were running out of water. They were feeling sick, exhausted. There was no help in sight."

I looked at him, and then back at the wall. Tobias was gone.

"Where did he go?" I asked.

"That's what the men wanted to know. They thought he'd run away. They couldn't blame him, if he wanted to save himself. But they didn't really know . . ."

Now on the wall I saw the head of the shadow dog lowered; I saw him creeping forward, inch by inch. Suddenly he sprang up and moved this way and that!

"He had crept away to get help. And then he ran, through bullets whizzing around him and the smoke from cannons." Streams of smoke from Grandpa's pipe were shadowed on the wall.

"It didn't get any easier when he was out of range. He had to run through mud and sand, through hot sun and dark night, with the moon swallowed by clouds." I heard a creak as the lantern was moved. The wall turned black.

"He had to run mile after mile."

The shadow came back on the wall, its mouth opening and closing. Panting.

"He ran and ran, until he found other soldiers, in a town far away. They were at a dance, and they didn't know about their friends. Tobias barked and barked at them. They tried to chase him away, but he came back. Once through the door, once through a window. Barking and barking."

On the wall, I saw the shadow of the dog barking as Grandpa talked.

"Finally, one soldier—the smartest of the bunch—believed that something was wrong. He ordered his men to follow Tobias.

"Tobias led them back many miles, all along the way he'd come." Now the shadow on the wall was moving slower. I could tell his breathing was coming out like pieces of rag, that his two front legs were wobbly.

"He's tired," I said.

"He can't give up," said Grandpa.

I watched him moving across the wall. "What happened?"

"Well, they found the soldiers who were pinned down. There was a terrible fight with the enemy." The lantern flared, and there were more puffs of smoke on the wall.

33

"All the soldiers were saved."

I nodded. "And what happened to Tobias?"

Grandpa looked at me, it seemed like a long time. Then he smiled. "Oh, he was okay," said Grandpa. "After it was over, it was his turn to dance."

I saw the shadow of the dog jumping across the wall.

"Now, look here," said Grandpa.

I looked over at him, and saw his hands set together, one on top of the other.

"The thing about Tobias, see, is that he's a dog. He's not a wild animal. And what is it about dogs?"

"They're friendly," I said.

"That's right. They're tame. And you can tame Tobias."

He showed me how to form my hands. It wasn't too hard, once you got the trick of it. Once you figured out where you had to leave a little space for the eye, and you got comfortable with opening your fingers to make the mouth open and close.

After a little while, I saw my Tobias on the wall.

"So how's that?" he asked.

I made Tobias bark.

"I can see he likes you already," said Grandpa.

I put my hands down. "Grandpa," I said. "That little boy you knew. Was he one of the soldiers when he grew up?"

He looked at me, puffing his pipe. "He was the smartest one of all," he said.

6

THERE WAS a cold snap in the middle of July.
With a lot of rain. Uncle Edward said autumn
was trying to bully its way into summer. I
thought of it as a big fight I couldn't see, up
behind the clouds. But I knew no matter what
happened in the short run, autumn would even-
tually win; then my mother would have a job
and I'd be living with her again.

I always passed a horse on the way back home
from the store. He was black in front, but in the
back he was white and dappled with black spots.
Like whoever had painted him black had run out
of paint and done the best they could with the
rest.

He always stayed away from the fence when
I walked by. When the cold snap came, he

seemed restless. I stood by the fence and watched him running, tossing his head. I had some grass, but I didn't know much about horses. I didn't know if it was the right kind of grass. My mother had told me they were shy, unnatural creatures, best kept away from. She knew a boy when I was little who was kicked in the head by one, and was never right in his mind from that day on.

I hadn't run into those kids again on my walks back home from the store, but now I saw them ahead, standing on the riverbank, throwing stones in the water. The river was swollen up from all the rain. The tree that had fallen was washed over in more spots, and it seemed to shift a little in the rush of the water. I didn't know if even Robert would like it.

The two younger kids were just lobbing the stones in, but the older kid was throwing them overhand, aiming at the rocks that showed in the river. I could see one hit sometimes and skip off in a wild direction.

They all stopped throwing when they saw me. The younger boy and girl just stared. But the older boy broke into that wide grin of his.

At school my mother always said to kids when she caught them fighting, "Now, you could have just walked away." So I was going to walk past.

Like I hadn't seen them, even though they already saw that I had.

Then I got the idea.

I turned back and started down the bank. They had already turned around and were throwing stones in the water again. Then the little girl saw me, as she stood up with a big rock.

"Davey," she said.

The older kid faced me. He grinned again. Now I could see his tooth.

"Going to walk the log?" he said. The top of the tree was shuddering from the force of the river.

"I want to show you a trick," I said. My heart was pounding again, like it had on the log.

"What kind of trick?" he asked.

"A different trick than the log," I said. "Even that little girl walked the log."

He wasn't grinning now. "Well, show it."

"Tonight," I said. "Up at my aunt's house."

"What kind of trick is it you can't show now?"

"You'll have to see," I said. Then I walked back up the bank.

After supper, I walked out on the porch and found them in the yard. The little girl's face was lit as she looked up at the windows. I didn't see the two boys at first, then I did. They were trying to jump on the wheelbarrow that was standing on its end in the ground. Trying to jump up and hold on to the handles and balance there.

When they saw me, they stopped and walked into the light from the house.

"Just a second," I said.

Davey only stared.

I went back into the house. Aunt Elena and Uncle Edward were still sitting in the kitchen having their coffee. Real quiet, I took a lantern and a box of matches out of the living room and brought them to the porch.

"What's he gonna do, Davey?" said the little boy.

Davey watched while I set the lantern down and lit it, the way I'd seen Grandpa do. The flame popped, and then burned steady.

I laced my fingers together and stretched out my hands. I tried to remember exactly the way I'd practiced it all afternoon. Then I sat next to the lantern.

"Now, look over here at the wall," I said.

"I don't see nothin' there," said Davey. He was grinning again.

I put my hands up, the way Grandpa had showed me.

"Hey, it's a dog," said the little girl.

My Tobias was on the wall. Davey watched

him, and looked at my hands, trying to see how I'd done it. But I kept my hands moving. I kept Tobias barking, and cocking his head. It wasn't as good as Grandpa's, but it wasn't bad, either. You could make out what he was doing, all right.

"Now, this here dog is named Tobias," I said. I saw the little girl mouth his name. So I made Tobias look at her, and then at the other boy, and then at Davey.

"And the thing that's special about Tobias is, he saved a bunch of men once."

"Okay, show me how you do it," said Davey. He was walking toward the porch.

"You haven't seen the whole thing yet," I said. The littler boy looked over at me and then at Davey. Davey seemed to think it over. He stopped walking and folded his arms.

"You see, Tobias was the mascot of a bunch of men who worked in the factory. They gave him their food. He stayed up late with them when they worked all night."

I made Tobias bark then. "He wants me to get to the good part," I said.

"Well, one night there was this fire in the factory," I said. "It started out small, but it got bigger and bigger. It got so hot it sealed the doors shut. And all the men were trapped." I made Tobias look around, afraid. "Even Tobias."

"What happened?" said the little girl.

"Shut up," said Davey. Then he looked at me.

"Well, Tobias found a hole in the side of the factory. Just big enough for him. And he crawled out. And then he kept crawling, until he got farther away, where the fire wasn't shooting out flames and pieces of glass and stuff, and he got up and ran. He ran and ran, until he got to a village. Everyone in the village was at a . . . at a party. And he led them back; he ran and ran." I was making Tobias move across the wall, back and forth and back and forth. "And he brought them there, and they put out the fire. And he saved them." I looked from one to the other. "He saved everyone, every one of them."

Nobody spoke for a while. Then Davey said, "There's no dog could really do that."

"There was," I said.

"Was not," said Davey.

"Was not," said the little boy.

Then Davey grinned at me. "Old goofy story," he said.

My face got hot. I stood up and I could feel my heart pounding. There was a strange taste in my mouth.

Davey took a step forward. I could see the little girl, biting her lip.

"Jamie." It was Aunt Elena's voice, behind me. I couldn't move. "Jamie," she said again. Then

42

I turned around. Aunt Elena was standing in the doorway. "Jamie honey, could I talk to you for a second?"

I looked back at Davey, and then I went inside.

"It's all right for you to have your friends here," she said. "But it wasn't right for you to take out the lantern and light it without asking us."

I could see Davey grinning through the screen. I looked up at her. "Grandpa did it," I said.

Her mouth got into that tight line again. "Let's not bring him into this," she said. "What if it tipped over?"

I looked down.

"Now, it isn't safe. And you know your mama told us to take extra good care of you. To be sure and keep a close eye on you."

"Seems like everybody is," I said.

"Now, don't you smart-answer me. There's people, and maybe you're one of them, that needs to be watched." She took a deep breath and turned away. Then she looked at me again. "Now listen. I suppose if you want to go out and play, well, then, that's all right. I'll just be sending out Uncle Edward."

I nodded. Then I turned and went back outside.

The kids had gone.

The lantern was sitting there, solid as a rock. I sat down next to it.

Just for the hang of it, I put my hands together and made Tobias. He came out so clear. And it was funny, it must have been the light, it being outside. But for the couple of minutes I was alone, he seemed to be doing things I didn't make him do.

7

ONE NIGHT at supper, in late July, Aunt Elena said she had something to ask me. There was the sound of us chewing, and the crickets, and now there was just the crickets. She said there was a Saturday antiques show they had a chance to go to, at the fairgrounds in Philippi. A dealer in the next town would give them a ride to it. As it was a good distance, they would have to set out early, and wouldn't get home till dark. It'd be such a long and tiring trip, she said, that she thought it would be best if I just stayed around the house.

"And the truck," said Uncle Edward. "It'll be tight in the truck."

"Is that all right?" she asked.

"Yes, ma'am."

"Speak up, boy, if it's not," said Uncle Edward.

"It is all right," I said. Ever since Aunt Elena had given me my last talking-to, I had tried to do what she said. I knew I had displeased her, and would have displeased my mother, too, if she had known about it. And a fire, that would be the worst thing.

Saturday was a chilly, gloomy day. They had left me some bread and jam for breakfast, so I ate that. They had also wrapped up a ham sandwich in white paper and put it in the icebox. I ate that pretty soon after I finished my breakfast.

There was no sun, so there could be no shadows. I didn't want to think about lighting the lantern. I took out some of my mother's letters and read them over. I tried to pretend they were a new batch of letters I'd just received.

I went and sat on the front porch.

I watched a squirrel take a few steps, and stop. And take a few steps more. If I could remember how he moved, later I could try to make a shadow of him.

Then I saw a man on a wagon pulled by a big gray horse. The wagon stopped in the road and the man stepped down. He took off his hat and peered at the house, and then at me.

46

"Grandpa!" I said. I was already running toward him.

He lifted me up when I reached him, and then sat me on the wagon. I told him how I was staying home the whole day.

"I thought they might be going to that fair," he said.

While he was climbing back up, I saw a crumpled paper tacked on the board in front of his seat. It was a circular for the antiques fair in Philippi.

After he settled down next to me, the gray horse in front turned his head sideways, so I could see the black square over his eye.

"Pirate horse," I said.

"How's that?"

"That black patch," I said.

Grandpa laughed. "That's a blinder," he said. "It keeps the horse looking straight ahead, so we can go about our work."

The horse walked ahead, and the wagon bumped over the road. There was some stuff in the back—a large, rusty spring, some pieces of wood, a scratched-up sink—and it rattled as we moved along.

"First stop," said Grandpa.

He turned the wagon down a narrow road. Pretty soon, we came to a small gray cabin with smoke coming out of its chimney. Grandpa pulled on the reins.

"Hello," called Grandpa.

A man with white hair appeared. He was wearing a ship captain's hat.

"Hello, Pete," said Grandpa.

"Hello, Darcy," said Pete.

Grandpa and I got down.

"Who's the new boss?" asked Pete.

"My grandson."

Pete nodded at me.

"Howdy, Pete," I said, and Grandpa laughed.

Grandpa said he and Pete had to haul something. He told me to stand by the front of the gray horse and hold on to his bridle. He said he'd probably be all right, but if some animal—especially a snake—showed up, he'd be off to the races.

While Pete and Grandpa walked to the cabin, I walked slow and careful to the horse. I lifted my hand to reach the bridle, and the horse moved his head. I put my hand down and took a step back. The two men were out of sight.

Then I lifted my hand real quick and caught hold of his bridle. He nodded his head. Then he settled down.

They came back, carrying a big metal box. One side of it was missing, and the top didn't fit square.

They counted to three, and I heard it crash into the wagon. The horse took a step forward, but I held tight to his bridle. Then Grandpa and Pete walked up to where I was holding the horse.

"Is he doin' a good job, Pete?" asked Grandpa.

Pete squinted. "He seems to be," he said. Then he winked at me.

We all shook hands, and then Grandpa and I got back on the wagon.

When we returned to the road, I asked him what was in the box.

"Nothing," said Grandpa. "Pete's got no use for it anymore."

"What do we do with it?"

"When the wagon's all loaded up, I take it over to Samuel Hayes and his brother Henry. And they buy it off of me."

"That's really good," I said.

"Yes," he said, and smiled. "Yes, I guess it is."

The rest of the morning, and into the afternoon, we picked up stuff. We got the base of an icebox from a man named Smitty, and a box of green bottles from a woman named Mary. We picked up a bunch of newspapers from a woman who lived near Aunt Elena and Uncle Edward's store, and Grandpa tied them up with string.

All that time, I slowly became friends with the horse, whose name was Sam. He'd let me pet his nose, and he'd nuzzle me under the arms and snort. I practiced the snort back at him, blowing out air through my mouth, letting my lips shake loose.

After we loaded up the papers, Grandpa said it was time for lunch.

"I ate my lunch this morning," I said.

"Could be time for another," he said.

Sam walked up the road from the store, going in the other direction from Aunt Elena's house. He walked past a gulley filled with ferns and thornbushes, and began to trot when we reached a patch of thick woods.

We came up over a rise, and then Grandpa turned the wagon off the road, down a narrow, rutted drive. We were bouncing up and down, and the things in back were making a terrible racket.

"I like this part the best," said Grandpa, and laughed.

We came to a little wooden house. There was cardboard stuck in some of the windows, where glass was broken out.

"Here we are," said Grandpa. "Best chow in West Virginia."

"What's this?" I asked.

"This is where I live," he said, and got down from the wagon.

He unhitched Sam and led him over to a bucket full of food. Then he went into the house, and I followed him.

It was one small room. There was a table and two chairs on one side. A bed and an overstuffed chair with its insides coming out on the other.

Grandpa was lighting a match by the stove.

"Dang stove," he said. "I'll mean to see to that flue." He blew out the match. He walked over to the icebox, opened the door, and peered inside.

"Don't get too much company these days," he said. He moved something inside the icebox. "But we're in luck."

He took out a plate with cheese on it. From a cupboard he brought out a loaf of bread. He cut off part of the bread with his jackknife, and walked to the door and threw it out. He sliced off some cheese and bread for me, and then he went to the shelf and got a jar of mustard that had little dark things in it.

"Those are whisker seeds," he said. "They'll grow whiskers on your chin."

"Come on, Grandpa," I said. He ruffled my hair with his hand.

He sat down and started to eat.

"What's wrong?" he asked.

"I'm kind of thirsty," I said.

"Of course, of course," he said. "Come to think of it, I am, too."

He brought out a jar of water from the icebox and put it in front of me. He took a bottle of whiskey from the shelf and poured some into a china cup, and put that in front of his plate.

Then he sat down and took a big bite of cheese and bread.

"That little boy you told me about. Did he ever come here and eat with you?"

He stopped chewing for a minute. Then he started chewing again. Then he said, "Not here. But someplace else."

"What was his name?" I asked.

"William," said Grandpa.

"William," I said. "William was my father's name."

"That's right," said Grandpa. "He was my son."

"I thought so," I said. Then I looked at him. "I know about all the stuff with the fire when I was little, how he was almost a hero, how he almost saved those men . . ."

"Where did you hear that?" he asked.

"Everybody knows it," I said. "But before that, when he was younger." I took a breath. "What was he like then?"

He seemed to be thinking real hard. Then he

spoke, but not like when he told the stories; now he spoke like each word had some weight to it, like each word was a little stone and he was placing it carefully on the table. "You could see a lot of hero in him," said my grandfather. "The way he rode. The way he cast a line. Not everybody could see it. But I could." He stared at the cup in front of him. He slid it a little ways away, and then slid it back where it had been. "You know, I raised him, him and your aunt, all by myself," he said. "I like to think I did a pretty good job."

"You did show him the shadows," I said.

He took a minute. "Sure I did," he said.

After lunch, Grandpa sat in his chair and said he was going to do some thinking with his eyes shut. I sat at the table for a while—I was thinking, too. Then I went over and sat down on the floor next to Grandpa's chair. I put my head against it and closed my eyes.

The next thing I knew, Grandpa was standing over me, shaking me awake.

He said, "Time to get you back. In fact, it's past that time."

Outside the cardboard and glass, it was gray.

It took a while to get Sam hitched up to the wagon. "He's part mule," Grandpa said. I had to help pull on his bridle, to force him back to the wagon traces.

It was starting to get dark by the time we set out for Aunt Elena's house.

"What time they say they were getting back?" he asked me.

"By dark," I said.

"Well, then, we're okay," said Grandpa.

Coming down the road past the store, Grandpa stopped the wagon. He got a lantern out from under the seat, lit it, and hooked it onto a rod that came up past the seat.

We bounced along, with the lantern swaying.

"Are you still practicing?" asked Grandpa.

"Yes," I said. "But I can still mainly just get Tobias."

"The others will come," he said.

I looked out ahead. Dark, with no lights. Off to the side, I could see a huge shadow of me cast by the swinging lantern. It rippled on the trees and grasses and disappeared when the land fell away.

"Now look over there," I said to Grandpa.

He turned and looked where I was pointing.

"That's the giant," I said. I waved my hands and shook my head from side to side, making my shadow move. Then it was gone; then back again.

"Hello, Giant," said Grandpa.

"His name is Bill," I said. "Bill the giant. He lives in the woods, at night . . . And he's not afraid of anything. And strong, boy, is he strong! He could lift up a whole tree if he wanted to, or all the stuff in this wagon, and carry it and put it down somewhere else."

"That's strong," said Grandpa.

I stood up in the wagon, and Grandpa reached for me. But then I managed to keep my balance while we rattled down the road toward the bridge. I could hardly see the shape of him in the river, and then I saw him again. My shadow was bigger now.

"Look how tall he is," I said.

Grandpa looked. Then he saw it. "Tall as a man," he said.

He let me stand there on the wagon, all along the road to Aunt Elena's house. Watching that big shadow.

8

AUNT ELENA and Uncle Edward were on the
porch when we pulled near. Uncle Edward was
holding a lantern up, and they were peering into
the darkness.

"It's okay," yelled Grandpa as he stopped the
wagon.

"Pa?" said Aunt Elena. "Jamie? Is he with
you?"

"I'm here," I said. Grandpa and I walked up
to the house.

"Praise God," said Aunt Elena. Then she shot
a look at me, like when she'd seen me with the
lantern.

"We were about to start out a search," said
Uncle Edward. "Where'd you find him?"

Grandpa looked at me. Then back at them.
"He was with me most of the day."

I saw Aunt Elena tighten her mouth the way she did, like a stitch pulling in a cloth.

"Jamie, you go on inside. You'll find some supper. I best have a word with you," she said to Grandpa.

She closed the door behind me. On the table there was a bowl of stew that had come from a can. It was still sort of warm. I picked up a fork, and then I heard the words from outside.

She said to Grandpa that he had done a very wrongful thing, taking me away on a day when they knew nothing about it. And then she said the thing again about keeping me closely watched. That was what my mother wanted, thank heaven, and even though it was a burden on her, she had to do it.

I was trying to pick the peas and carrots away from the meat while she talked. I was just wishing she wouldn't be cross with him. And then she said that he of anybody should understand that, with what had happened to my father. I put my fork down, and tried not to move.

"Jamie's been saying things," she said. "Once or twice. Letting on how his father had been some kind of soldier, some . . . wild lumberjack." It was quiet a second; I heard the wagon creak. "Of course he did act wild enough when he was young," she said. "Many was the time the two of you were out so late, the Lord knew where, while I kept supper. But then those high spirits of his you liked so much turned into real mischief, and his fanciful stories, well, he got to be a little too good at those."

And then she said what I'd heard before, back in our town, once in a store where a bunch of men were sitting around. And after they'd said it and seen me and hushed up, one had offered me a piece of hard candy and I'd taken it and walked away, their words still ringing in my ears.

She said she couldn't help but think his reckless ways had something to do with the fire— she knew no one liked to speak of it. So what was my grandfather building up in my mind? Telling me such stories about him, when they were worried enough I was going to take on his ways.

Suddenly his voice was louder than I'd ever heard it. "You've got no right—"

"It's you that's got no right," she said. "Keeping that boy out into the night, when not a soul knew. I seen how it happened once. I see how it turned out. I'm not gonna see it again . . . You shouldn't come by and visit him for a while."

"There's no one can stop me from seeing my grandson." I could hardly recognize his voice.

"Yes, there is, Pa," she said. "If it comes to

keeping him safe, we might have a thing or two to say to his mother."

I couldn't hear anything for a while.

Then I heard the horse and wagon drive away.

I didn't feel right the next morning. Aunt Elena felt my cheek. She didn't think I had a fever. But I hadn't eaten hardly anything the night before, or that morning either, so she said I should spend the day at the house and not go to the store, just to be on the safe side. She'd come back and check on me in the middle of the day.

I sat up in my bed and leafed through some magazines Aunt Elena subscribed to, which she had brought me to pass the time. There were pictures of new kitchen floors, and one had an ad for a floor sweeper that could stick its nose under a couch.

I took out the last letter I'd gotten from my mother. I read over the sentences near the end, written on her pale-blue paper:

The Teachers' Association tells me of a position opening up in a District outside of Hartford. They say that I would be a perfect match for it.

That meant I would be leaving soon, and that was good. I didn't want to stay here anymore.

When I folded up the letter to put it away, I noticed that the light coming in the window made a shadow of my hands on the wall. A shadow of my hands folding up that piece of paper.

I turned, so my legs were over the side of the bed, and I finished folding up the paper that way. I didn't want to see any shadows. Not Derek, or Robert, or Tobias, or Bill. It was a simple thing—even that boy Davey had seen it— but I just recognized it then.

Shadows had nothing to them at all.

9

I DIDN'T have a fever, but I didn't not have one, either. Aunt Elena couldn't exactly tell. I felt like I had a fever, but she said I didn't seem hot. She said there were a lot of people coming down with the grippe—she meant the flu—on account of the cold and wet weather we'd been having. She thought I must be coming down with it, or else having just a touch of it. In any case, the best thing for me was to do what I'd been doing—stay put and rest.

I kept waiting to get the word from my mother that she was sending for me. But I got only one letter from her, a short one that said she'd be having a meeting with the School Board of that district by Hartford. And then, not another word.

The night it happened I was feeling feverish again. Aunt Elena put her hand to my forehead and said I felt warm. She put me to bed earlier than usual. I could hear her and Uncle Edward's muffled voices from the kitchen, and see the gray light outside my window, before I fell asleep.

I didn't know what woke me. I would have sworn a kind of scratching sound, but when I sat up in bed I didn't hear anything. It was late, and they were asleep. There was a kind of pale light the color of cream coming in through the window. I sat up on the foot of my bed and looked out. There was a three-quarter moon in the sky, and rags of clouds were blowing by it.

On the wall next to my bed, away from the window, I could see my shadow. And then something else. And then just my shadow again.

I looked out the window. Maybe a bird had flown by, or a branch dipped down.

I lay down in my bed again and put the covers over me. I was feeling a chill all of a sudden. I closed my eyes to get to sleep.

And opened them again.

And I saw on the wall, for an instant, the fuzzy shadow of something.

I bolted up and looked out the window. I thought I might see a squirrel there, staring at me, but there was nothing. Just the moon and its creamy light coming in. I padded to the window and looked out. The meadow was empty. The fence was clear.

I was feeling more chills, so I got back into bed. But now I lay with my eyes open, looking at the wall.

After a little while, I saw the shadow again. It was fuzzy, like it was coming from a long way away. But it was a shadow. And I couldn't see what was casting it.

I lay there, holding still, and watched. As the shadow seemed to form itself, it slowly became more clear. It was flicking now, this way and that, and then sometimes it would slow down.

It was the head and front legs of a dog.

"Tobias . . ." I said.

The shadow stopped when I said that. Then it seemed to get excited; it moved back and forth across my wall.

I looked out the window.

"Grandpa?" I said. "Grandpa, are you there?" But the window was empty, and even though I could see the shadow, I could see nothing casting it.

The shadow seemed to get even clearer as I watched. "Hello, Tobias," I said softly. Suddenly I didn't care how he got there. I was just glad to see him.

The shadow ran back and forth on my wall. It disappeared. Then it came back, and its mouth opened and closed quickly. It was the same motion as when Grandpa had made him bark.

"Did you come to see me?" I said. He slowed down, and his snout was gone; there were shadows of two ears, as if he was facing me. Looking at me.

"What is it?" I asked, and now he got excited again, barking, running this way and that on my wall.

"Tell Grandpa I'm feeling fine," I said, but even as I said that, I could feel the chills go through me again.

The shadow dog kept running, back and forth, moving its mouth as if it was barking. Nothing I was saying seemed to be right. And then I thought back to the story Grandpa had told me, when he first showed me Tobias. How Tobias had run far away from the pinned-down soldiers and found another group of soldiers. And how they hadn't understood him at first . . .

"You want me to follow you," I said. And the shadow of the dog seemed more excited; it leapt on the wall.

I got out of bed. I took off my pajamas and pulled on a sweater and a pair of pants, socks and shoes. I looked back at the wall, and the shadow was gone. I went to the window, and for a second I thought I saw that shadow on the ground.

I walked quietly through the house and left by the front door.

Outside, it was cold, and there were drops of rain. I saw a shadow floating away from me, toward the road. Then the moon went behind a cloud, and I started to run as well. Following after him.

I caught glimpses of him when the moon came out. Part wolf was Tobias, Grandpa had said, and his shadow had become four-legged and large and fast. He ran ahead, and then I wouldn't see him, and then when the moon came out I'd see him running toward me, or waiting, or making his silent barks, to urge me on ahead.

The river was silver in the moonlight, on my right as I ran. Its rushing seemed to fill up the night with its sound.

I was running past the place where the tree had fallen when I didn't see Tobias ahead of me anymore. I stopped and my breath came out ragged. I wasn't cold now; I was sweating a lot. But as I looked ahead for the shadow of Tobias, I felt the chill start down my back again.

I looked behind me. And looked again. There was a misty shape on the bank. As I drew nearer,

I saw it was a shadow as well. A shadow in the shape of a very large cat.

"Robert!" I said, and the shadow cocked its head at me.

Quickly it moved to the edge of the fallen log. And then very slowly and very carefully, the shadow of the bobcat walked, first one paw and then the next, walked out onto the log that shuddered in the river.

"It'll be quicker," I said out loud. The shape of the big cat stopped and cocked its head at me. Then it walked forward again, paw before paw.

I walked down the bank. I slipped once, as I had done before. I got down to where the log met the bank and I looked out.

I could see the shadow ahead of me, out on the log. It looked misty again. The log was rocking in the rushing water, the moon was glinting off the rocks.

I put my hands out, the way I had in the store.

Foot before foot, I walked out on the log, watching the bobcat ahead of me. If I lost sight of him, I didn't know what I'd do.

When the log shifted, we stopped and swayed on it a little, side to side. When it settled, we started again.

I tried not to think how there was nothing on either side but the river.

When I reached the far bank, I climbed up, back to the road. I saw the shadow flick into the woods . . . and now Tobias was there, leaping, and silently barking. He must have run the long way, over the bridge. Faster than I could have.

He took off ahead of me, and I ran after him.

I knew we were going to Grandpa's house. I was trying to remember the way.

The moon came and went. When we got to the place where the gulley ran off the side of the road and the woods turned thick, it went behind a big bank of clouds and stayed there.

I ran on, but I couldn't see a thing. I remembered how Tobias couldn't stop, and I couldn't either. But I was running blind. That was when he came back for me, and I heard him panting at my side. And then a fluttering of wings coming down for us, and rising high in the air to get a look, and then swooping down for us again. The wings of a hawk named Derek. Showing us the way through the dark.

I had to half run and half walk at the end. When I got to Grandpa's house, at the bottom of that little road, I saw a lantern lit inside. But it looked fuzzy, too. When I got inside, I knew why. There was a kind of funny air inside that seemed thick, and smoke was coming from the stove.

Grandpa was lying in bed, on his back.

"Grandpa!" I yelled, but it came out more like a cough. He didn't move. I shook him, and he fell back the way he'd been. I looked around, and I couldn't see any of the shadows that had brought me there. I wanted to cry, but I didn't have time. I knew I had to get him out of that smoky air. I put my hands under his arms and dragged him off the bed. I dragged him across the floor as best I could. And it wasn't until I got him outside and I stood up that I saw the shadow next to me—cast by the moon, or maybe not—the tall shadow of Bill, who had lent me his strength to pull a man to safety from a fire.

10

GRANDPA WAS already sitting up and breathing—shaky at first—when Aunt Elena and Uncle Edward pulled up in a car. As the lights swept toward us over the ground, I swore I could see those shadows looking on. Then the lights passed and I couldn't see them anymore.

It seemed something had woken my aunt and uncle. Aunt Elena said it was a sound like a bird thumping against the window, and Uncle Edward said it was something scrambling on the roof. They'd gotten up and seen I was gone and figured maybe somehow I'd gone to Grandpa's. They borrowed Mrs. Morgan's old Chevy from next door.

They didn't say too much when they got there. They looked as if they were still trying to figure out what happened but didn't want to ask me yet. They bundled us both into the back seat of the car and took us to Dr. Parker's house. He saw Grandpa for a while, and then he took me into a bare room with a cot and a sink and looked in my eyes and down my throat, and listened to my chest through his stethoscope.

He walked with me out to the little waiting room he had by his office. His wife had brought out a pot of tea, and Grandpa was drinking some. Dr. Parker poured a cup for me. He told us all that Grandpa had had smoke inhalation, but that he would be fine. The flue in his old stove had backed up and filled the room with smoke while he was sleeping.

Dr. Parker said I seemed none the worse for wear.

When we got back in the car, Aunt Elena didn't say anything for a while. Then I heard a funny sound. She was crying. "I see I don't understand a thing," she said.

Grandpa leaned forward and put his hand on her shoulder. Then he put his other arm around me.

My mother got that job. She came down a week later. She came on one of the days I was helping Grandpa, so I didn't see her till late in the afternoon. I guess she had had a long talk with Aunt Elena by the time we pulled up to Aunt Elena's house.

She ran up while I was sitting on the wagon, holding the reins to Sam. She stopped a couple of feet away. Grandpa took the reins, and I got down from the wagon. She seemed to pull in her breath.

"You've gotten taller," she said.

I smiled at that. The way Grandpa always smiled when you said something he liked.

"You want to see what we got?" I said. And I showed her the stuff in the back of the wagon.

The day before we left, Grandpa and I took a walk along the river. It was down some. You could see more rocks in places.

We just walked along, without saying too much. Once in a while, Grandpa would pick up a stone and skip it three, four, five times. I skipped a couple myself.

"Well, what do you know," I said. We had gotten to the place where the tree had been across the river.

"What is it?" asked Grandpa.

"Used to be a log there," I said. "I guess it washed away."

He was staring out at the river.

"It was the log I walked that night," I said.

72

He turned and looked at me, and his eyes were watery.

"I can't get over how you came just then," he said.

"Sure, you know," I said.

"Know what?"

"About the shadows," I said.

"The shadows?"

"All the ones you showed me."

He just looked at me.

"When you told me the stories," I said. "When you were telling me about my father."

Grandpa pursed his lips. He sat down on a rock and started to take out his pipe. "About those stories . . ." he said.

"Oh, I know," I said. "I heard what Aunt Elena said to you. That he wasn't all those things.

But I figured he was, in a way." I looked right at him, so he'd understand. "Like the shadows. They really came for me that night."

He was looking back at me, listening.

"They really came," I said. "That's how I knew."

He didn't say anything then. He just leaned forward and hugged me.

I said goodbye to him at the station. Everyone was there. Uncle Edward ruffled my hair, and Aunt Elena kneeled down and drew me to her. Then she held me at arm's length, searching my face, like it wasn't just me who was leaving.

I walked over to Grandpa, and when I reached him I stuck out my hand.

He smiled when he shook it. And I smiled back.

Then I turned and walked with my mother onto the train, half dragging one of the suitcases she'd brought.

After we pulled out from the station and were going awhile, she asked me if I was okay. I nodded. I guess she'd seen there were some tears in my eyes, but I wasn't sad. Not really sad at all. I put my face to the window, and for every barn, for every tree, I saw a shadow it made, all of them stretching as far as I could see, on our way North.